SUPER CITIES!



# CHARLESTON

by Diane Lindsey Reeves

arcadia
CHILDREN'S BOOKS

**Published by Arcadia Children's Books**
A Division of Arcadia Publishing
Charleston, SC
www.arcadiapublishing.com



First published 2022

Manufactured in the United States of America.

ISBN 978-1-4671-9892-9

Library of Congress Control Number: 2022937948



Produced by Shoreline Publishing Group LLC
Santa Barbara, California
Designer: Patty Kelley

# Contents

# WELCOME TO Charleston!

It is easy to love a city like Charleston. Full of history, nature, and southern hospitality, Charleston welcomes millions of people every year. Many of these visitors come back to stay—more than 12,000 people move to the area annually!

Over the past 350 years, the city has had quite a story to tell. Full of beautifully preserved buildings and rich in history, the city is often called a "living museum." With old forts and dungeons, and sprawling plantations and historic mansions, Charleston landmarks tell stories about some of the best—and worst—parts

FAST FACTS

**Charleston, South Carolina**

**POPULATION: 150,277**

**REGIONAL POPULATION: 799,636**

**FOUNDED: 1670**

**NICKNAMES: Chucktown, Holy City, CHS**

of American history. The whole area is also a natural wonderland! Look out to sea from Charleston's amazing bridges. Drive down roads lined with towering oak trees draped in Spanish moss. Breathe in the smell of pluff mud at low tide. Watch the antics of pelicans, egrets, ibis, and other shorebirds. Watch dolphins swimming by in search of supper. Don't be surprised if you happen upon a lazy alligator or two. And take good care of the sea turtle nests! Those babies are so cute!

Turn the page to start exploring Charleston's fascinating story.

# CHARLESTON: Map It!

Charleston is a peninsula on the East Coast of the United States, in eastern South Carolina. The city surrounds Charleston Harbor, an inlet of the Atlantic Ocean where the Ashley, Cooper, and Wando Rivers come together. The city includes West Ashley, and Johns, James, and Daniel Islands. The wider area is known as the Lowcountry.

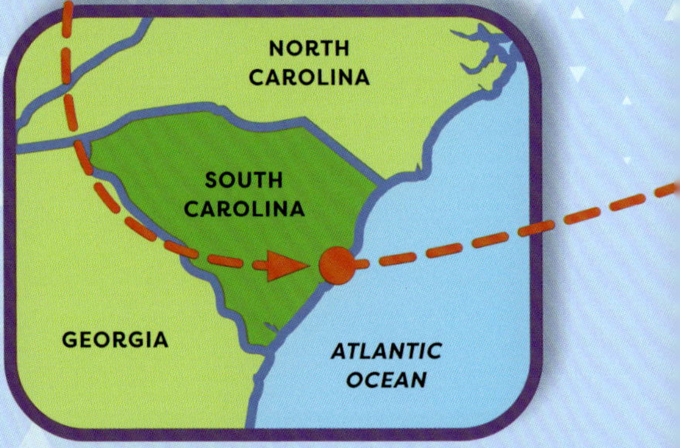

# Charleston, South Carolina

# A Seaport City

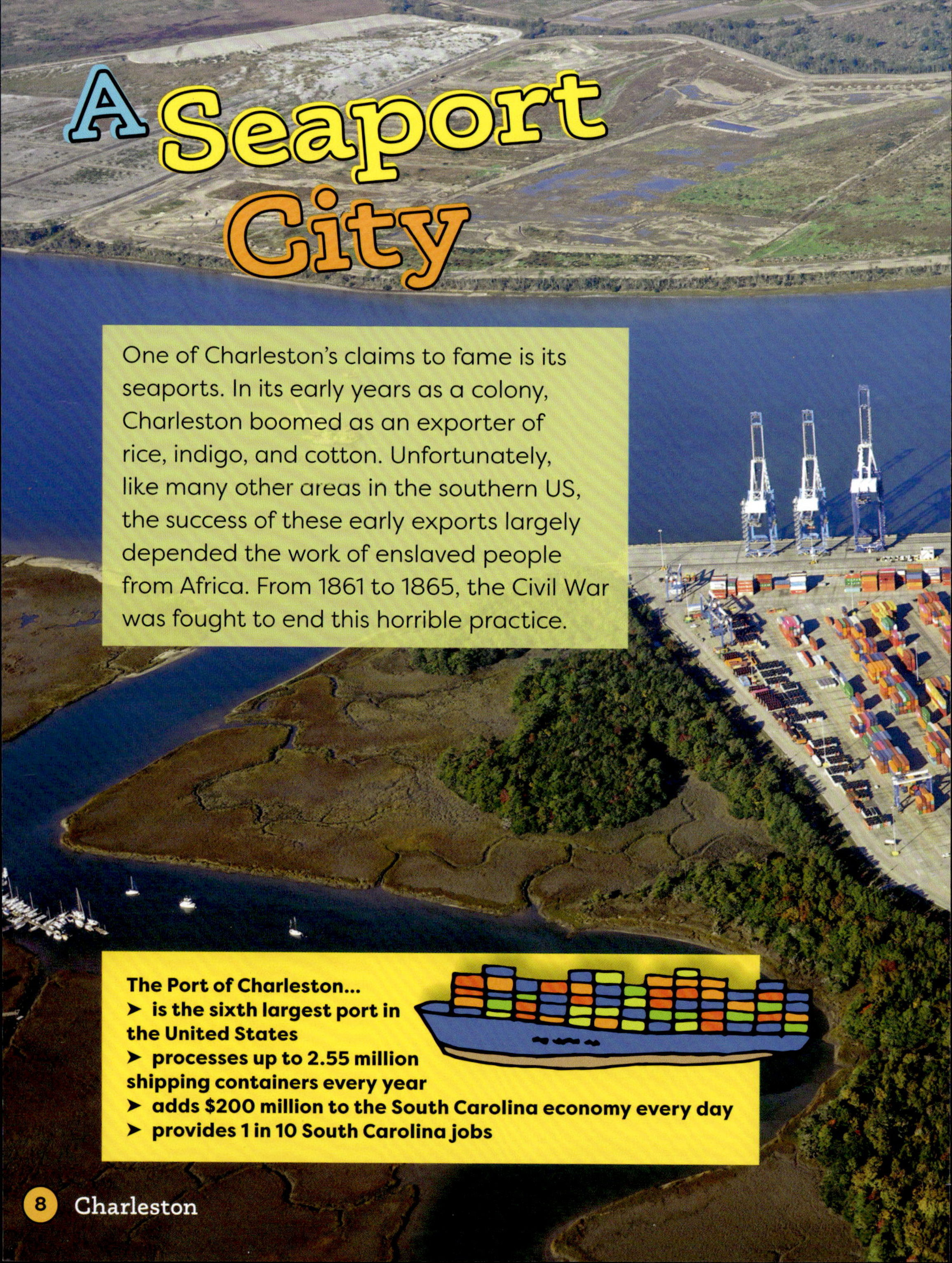

One of Charleston's claims to fame is its seaports. In its early years as a colony, Charleston boomed as an exporter of rice, indigo, and cotton. Unfortunately, like many other areas in the southern US, the success of these early exports largely depended the work of enslaved people from Africa. From 1861 to 1865, the Civil War was fought to end this horrible practice.

**The Port of Charleston...**

- **is the sixth largest port in the United States**
- **processes up to 2.55 million shipping containers every year**
- **adds $200 million to the South Carolina economy every day**
- **provides 1 in 10 South Carolina jobs**

**FAST FACTS**

**Import** = to bring products in from another country to be sold

**Export** = to send products to another country to sell

Charleston's harbor was left in tatters after the war, and the Southern economy had little to export. The seaports were quiet, as the city began the slow and painful process of rebuilding itself.

It took more than a hundred years for Charleston to reclaim its place as one of America's busiest seaports. Today, huge container ships carry thousands of products to and from Charleston's shores. Everything from furniture, clothes, and toys to auto parts, vehicles, and food products make their way around the globe from Chucktown's port.

# City of Bridges

Charleston is surrounded by water on almost every side. And where you find busy waterways, you find bridges! Charleston is home to a fascinating mix of bridges that includes everything from cable suspension bridges to drawbridges.

**Double Draw Bridge:** The Wappoo Creek Bridge connects West Ashley to James Island. It first opened to the public in 1956 and is named after the indigenous Wappoo people. The bridge raises up to let huge container ships pass underneath.

**The Big One!:** The star of Charleston's bridge line-up is the Arthur Ravenel Jr. Bridge. It opened in 2005 after five years of construction. The bridge crosses the Cooper River and connects Charleston with the town of Mount Pleasant. It stretches for 1,541 feet (470 m) across the water. The bridge surface is 200 feet (61 m) above the water and has two 600-foot (181-m) towers. It has eight lanes for cars, and a path for pedestrians and bicycles. It replaced the old Cooper River Bridge and was named for a longtime Charleston politician.

**Hello, Mount Pleasant:** The Don N. Holt Bridge is a three-span bridge crossing the Cooper River. It connects Daniel Island and Mount Pleasant to North Charleston.

**Swing It!** The Ben Sawyer Bridge connects the town of Mount Pleasant with Sullivan's Island. It is a swing bridge that spins sideways to let tall boats pass. The bridge was originally built in 1945 but was badly damaged by Hurricane Hugo in 1989. It was later repaired.

# NAMING CHARLESTON

The first non-Native people to settle Charleston were colonists from Great Britain. They had arrived from Bermuda, another British colony, and settled on the west bank of the Ashley River in 1670.

The colonists named their new city after British King Charles II (Charles's town, get it?). He became king in 1660 after the English Civil War. Charles II's father, Charles I, of course, was killed in that war and the nation was briefly led by a man named Oliver Cromwell—not a king. But Cromwell died in 1660 and English people brought back a king—Chucky the Second.

The new colonists had a good reason to name their city for their king. He had given them the land! (Of course, unfortunately, the English had stolen it from indigenous people in the first place.) Charles II gave Lord Anthony Ashley Cooper and seven other men control over the New World between Virginia, a British colony, and Spanish Florida. This was the area now known as North and South Carolina. The city was first called Charles Towne before being shortened to its current name in 1783.

**Lord Ashley Cooper (and yes, that's a wig)**

**King Charles II, Charleston's namesake (that's a wig, too)**

# CHARLESTON TODAY

Charleston is a survivor. Wars, enslavement, hurricanes, disease . . . through the years, all of these problems took a toll on Charleston. There were times that the city was down for the count, and it seemed like all was lost. Yet with each new challenge the people of Charleston fought back, learned from their mistakes, and found new ways to thrive.

Today the city stands as a reminder of things that should never ever happen again and an inspiration for how a place can emerge bigger and better than ever before. It is now a vibrant city that buzzes with high-tech energy, an entrepreneurial spirit, and a warm welcome for all who come its way.

Charleston often tops lists of best cities to visit in the United States and even the world. More than seven million people visit this super city every year. What is it that brings all these people to this charming coastal spot? Keep reading to find out!

**The Beaches!**
Charleston is home to several beautiful beaches. Take your pick of Folly Beach, Isle of Palms, Sullivan's Island, and Kiawah.

**The Nature!**
Shem Creek Park is a favorite nature spot near Charleston. Walk the boardwalks, explore the creek, and enjoy the wetlands. With a little luck, you'll spot a pod of dolphins swimming by.

## Shop 'til You Drop!

King Street is the place to go for antiques, good food, and trendy shops.

## The History!

A visit to Charleston is not complete without a horse-drawn carriage ride. Where else can you see 350 years of history in an hour-long tour?

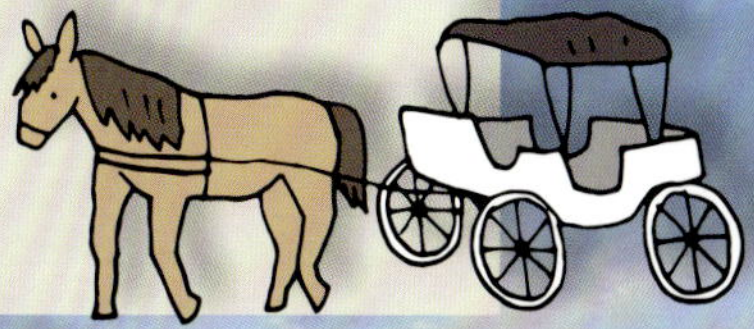

## The Food!

People come from all over the world to enjoy Charleston's tasty cuisine. From biscuits and sweet tea to shrimp and grits and fried green tomatoes, there is something sure to please everyone. But nothing says Charleston quite like an oyster roast.

# HISTORY: First People

Charleston was home to Native American tribes long before Europeans even knew that the "new world" existed. The southern half of what is now Charleston County was home to the Muskogean Nation which included the Ashepoo, Bohicket, Cofitachiqui, Combahee, Coosa, Cusabo, Cusso, Edisto, Escamacu, Etiwan, Kiawah, Kusso-Natchez, Stono, Wando, Wimbee, and Yamassee peoples. The Siouan tribes of Chicora, Pee Dee, Sampit, Santee, Sewee, Waccamaw, and Winyah lived in the northern Charleston area all the way up to what became North Carolina.

Little is known about the customs and culture of these early tribes. Clues to their language, lifestyle, and habits are few and far between. One important archaeological dig found the remains of a settlement at Santa Elena. That was a village set up by Spanish explorers, but evidence of indigenous people was also found there.

Many of the tribes moved, or migrated, from one area to another based on the seasons. They stayed near the coast during the warm weather months of spring and summer. They moved inland during the autumn and winter seasons. They were big on hunting, fishing, and gathering food.

Smallpox was a disease that arrived with European settlers. With no natural immunity to fight it, the disease killed many Native Americans. Over many years, some tribes lost as many as two-thirds of their people due to smallpox.

A map made in 1721 by an indigenous artist showed the names and sizes of tribes in the area. On the left is the English settlement of Charles Towne.

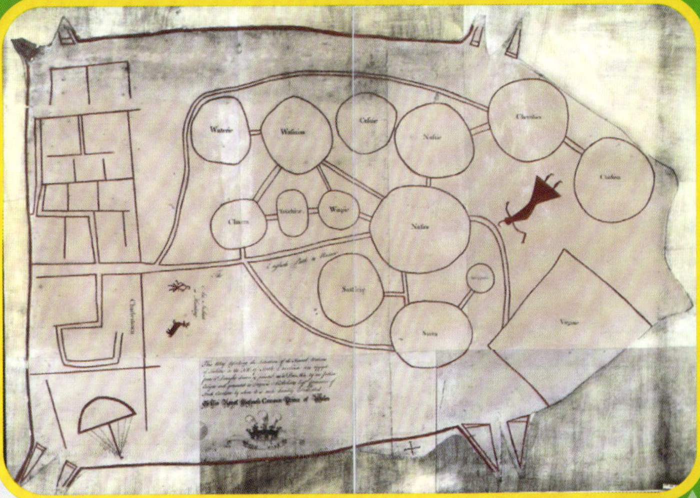

Many of the tribes that once lived in Charleston are now extinct. Some, including people of the Catawba, Pee Dee, Chicora, Edisto, Santee, Yamassee, Chicora-Waccamaw, and Cherokee, still live in South Carolina today.

**Charles Towne Landing** is where the first English settlers arrived in Charleston. It is now a state park and hosts various programs to show how settlers and Native Americans tried to coexist.

# HISTORY: Colonial Days

**1670:** Colonial Charles Towne was established in 1670 by 150 English settlers from Bermuda. They settled on the west bank of the Ashley River. In 1672, the colony moved to a more strategic peninsula between the Ashley, Cooper, and Wando Rivers.

**1680:** Charles Towne had grown into the fifth largest city in the North American colonies. This is thanks in part to Anthony Ashley Cooper, a loyal pal of King Charles II. He oversaw turning the colony into a great port. The new colony became prosperous by exporting rice and indigo (a plant used to dye clothes).

Charles Towne was the first American colony to use city planning. Streets were laid out in "broad and . . . straight lines." Most early US city streets followed old horse or walking trails.

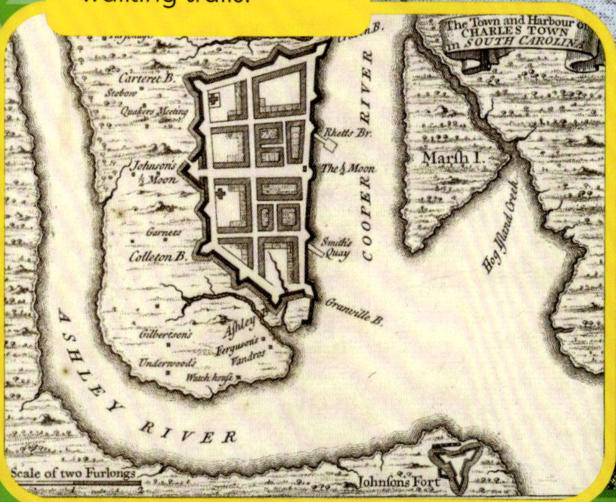

Charles Towne's colonists endured more than their fair share of trouble in the early years. They faced yellow fever (1699 and other years), smallpox epidemics (1711 and 1760), a plague among cattle (1730s), a fire that wiped out a third of the colony in just four hours (1740), and terrible storms and hurricanes (many!).

The colony had many enemies at first. The French, the Spanish, pirates, and of course, the indigenous people whose land they were taking, attacked by land and sea.

Early Charleston protected itself by building a wall around the colony. It was made from brick, palmetto logs, and tabby (a kind of cement made from oyster shells), and it stood until after the American Revolution. A few parts of the wall can still be seen around town.

Finished in 1713, this powder magazine—a place to hold gunpowder—is the oldest building still standing in South Carolina.

# HISTORY: Pirate Days!

Charles Towne was a big draw for pirates from its very beginning. It was a favorite hangout of famous pirates like Blackbeard, Stede Bonnet, and Anne Bonny.

FAST FACT

Weird but true. Blackbeard was said to light slow-burning cannon fuses in his beard to scare his enemies and show off his toughness.

**April 1718:** Blackbeard (real name: Edward Teach . . . maybe!), sailed into Charleston Harbor with a mission: He needed medicine for his crew. Being a pirate, he was not going to pay for it—instead, he took hostages until he got his way. Mission accomplished, he left after a week. Blackbeard was greatly feared from one end of the Atlantic Coast to the other. Yet, there is no evidence that he ever killed anyone until his last battle.

**May 1718:** Stede Bonnet teamed up with Blackbeard and arrived in Charleston in May 1718. Bonnet was known as the gentleman pirate. He was a rich kid born in Barbados but left the family plantation to pursue life on the high seas. Other pirates made fun of Bonnet for buying his first pirate ship instead of stealing it.

**November 1718:** Blackbeard met a gruesome end in a battle with a British naval officer named Robert Maynard.

**December 1718:** Bonnet was captured on Sullivan's Island. He was hanged for his crimes at the Battery in Charleston on December 10, 1718.

**Anne Bonny:** Anne Bonny was also a famous pirate. She did her dirty work in the Caribbean after growing up in Charleston. Bonny was a troublemaker even before she became a pirate. Her father did not like her first husband, so she set her dad's land on fire. When in battle as a pirate, Bonny dressed as a man. Legends say that Bonny returned to Charleston in her late twenties to live out the rest of her life.

# HISTORY: The American Revolution

**1773:** Charleston held its own version of the Boston Tea Party to protest the Tea Act from Great Britain. Instead of dumping crates of tea into the harbor, local colonists put it under lock and key in the Exchange and Custom House.

**June 1776:** On June 28, the British Navy attacked Fort Sullivan in Charles Towne. Outmanned and outgunned, the colonists still won the first big Southern battle of the American Revolution, which had started a year earlier in Massachusetts. Their secret weapon? Palmetto trees! The fort was fortified with super-strong, super-flexble palmetto logs. Cannonballs bounced off the logs!

**August 1776:** At the Exchange and Custom House, the colony of South Carolina declared its independence from England on August 5.

**1780:** It took three years, but the British came back to Charles Towne with even more men and firepower. They avoided Fort Moultrie by coming in from a different direction. On May 7, the two sides fought a fierce battle, but the British won.

**South Carolina's Colonel Francis Marion**, known as the Swamp Fox, used unusual "hit and run" tactics to outsmart the British Army. In 1780 and 1781, his ragtag militia would sneak in, strike hard, and take off before the British knew what hit them. Marion credited local indigenous people for inspiring his tactics.

# HISTORY: Before the Civil War

The antebellum era covered the years before the Civil War. (*Antebellum* means "before the war" in Latin). It was a time of growth and prosperity in the area. Cotton was king and indigo was queen in Charleston. Rice was so big that it made Charleston one of the richest cities in the world. But like many other Southern states, the main way that the economy grew was through the forced labor of enslaved African Americans.

**1740s:** While managing her family's farm near Charleston, Elizabeth Lucas Pinckney (page 32) led the way in making indigo a key cash crop for the area. The plant was used to dye fabric and brought millions of dollars to South Carolina.

**1822:** Denmark Vesey, a formerly enslaved person, tried to lead a rebellion of other enslaved people. Sadly, the rebellion was put down and Vesey was hanged. His actions made him a hero to people fighting slavery.

**1793:** After Eli Whitney invented the cotton gin in 1793, even more cotton was grown in Charleston. Using the machine, cotton was easier to harvest so planters grew more. More cotton meant more people to harvest it. The use of enslaved people throughout the South became one of the main causes of the Civil War.

**1842:** Famous author Edgar Allen Poe was an important literary figure in antebellum Charleston. In 1842, he wrote a famous story called *The Gold Bug* about buried treasure on Sullivan's Island.

The homes of enslaved people are preserved at Boone Hall Plantation.

## FAST FACT

A plantation was a large farm that used enslaved people to harvest crops. Charleston County was home to more than 300 plantations in the 1700s and 1800s, where tens of thousands of African people were enslaved.

**By 1860,** states in the North wanted southern states to stop using enslaved people for their labor. But southern states believed their way of life could not exist without enslaving people. On December 20, 1860, South Carolina became the first state to secede, or leave, the United States and join the newly formed Confederate States of America. Ten more states would join South Carolina.

# HISTORY: The Civil War

**1861:** On April 12, the first shots of the Civil War were fired from Fort Sumter in Charleston. The war pitted the United States against the Confederacy and killed nearly 620,000 Americans.

**1861:** On December 11, Charleston saw more destruction during the Great Fire that than it had from war battles. The fire burned more than 540 acres, 575 homes, many businesses, and five churches.

**1862:** On September 22, President Abraham Lincoln issued the Emancipation Proclamation. When it went into effect on January 1, 1863, this act freed enslaved people living in the Confederate states. However, the Union would have to win the Civil War to enforce this law.

**1863:** Charleston was a key target for both the Union army and navy, which began a long siege of the city on July 10.

**1864:** On February 17, the Confederate *Hunley* became the first submarine to ever sink a warship: it took down the Union ship *USS Housatonic* in Charleston Harbor. Not long after, the *Hunley* also sank. Its wreckage was not found until 1995.

**1865:** After enduring 587 days of bombardment, Confederate Charleston finally surrendered to the Union. The city fell on February 18, just a month and a half before the war ended. The Civil War officially ended on April 9, when Robert E. Lee surrendered the last major Confederate army to Ulysses S. Grant at the Appomattox Courthouse in Virginia.

**1865:** On April 15—just six days after the war ended—President Abraham Lincoln was assassinated by John Wilkes Booth.

# HISTORY: Charleston Rebuilds

After the Civil War ended, Charleston began to pick up the pieces. This period of history is known as the Reconstruction and lasted until 1877. After Lincoln was killed, Andrew Johnson became president of the United States. He was a southerner who believed in states' rights and wanted to make it easy for southern states to rejoin the Union. Congress did not always agree. Johnson vetoed so many bills passed by Congress that he became known as the "veto president."

**1865:** On December 6, the states ratified the 13th Amendment to the Constitution, which abolished slavery in America.

**Even after the war, cotton continued to be an important crop in South Carolina. Ships from port carried bales around the world.**

**1865:** The first high school for Black students was founded in Charleston by the New York-based American Missionary Association (AMA). It trained teachers and prepared freed enslaved people for careers and leadership. (The building still stands; in 1985, it became the Avery Research Center for African American History and Culture at the College of Charleston.)

**1868:** South Carolina adopted a new state constitution during a convention in Charleston. Two-thirds of the delegates were Black, including many formerly enslaved people. South Carolina was readmitted to the Union on July 9. It was, once again, officially part of the United States of America.

**1872:** Francis Lewis Cardozo was born free in Charleston in 1836. He became the first Black man to hold a statewide office in the United States when he was elected Secretary of State in South Carolina.

**1886:** Charleston was hit by a major earthquake on August 31. Thousands of buildings were damaged and 60 people were killed.

# HISTORY: The 1900s

**1901:** The Charleston Navy Yard opened to build and repair naval warships. For the next 90 years, the Navy Yard produced ships for the US Navy, including the USS *Tidewater* and USS *Bryce Canyon*. It was especially busy during World War II, when more than 26,000 people worked there.

**1919:** On May 10, the Charleston Riot broke out when five white sailors thought they were cheated by a Black man. Within an hour, the fight had grown to more than 1,000 sailors fighting Black people in the business district on King Street. At the time, it was the worst violence Charleston had seen since the Civil War.

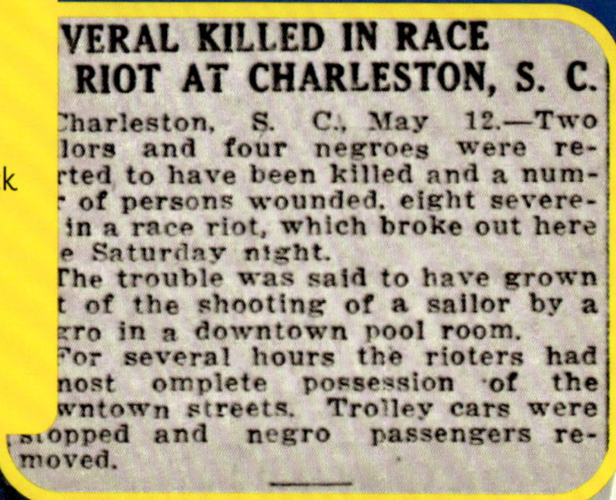

VERAL KILLED IN RACE RIOT AT CHARLESTON, S. C.

Charleston, S. C., May 12.—Two lors and four negroes were re- rted to have been killed and a num- of persons wounded, eight severe- in a race riot, which broke out here e Saturday night.

The trouble was said to have grown t of the shooting of a sailor by a gro in a downtown pool room.

For several hours the rioters had nost omplete possession of the wntown streets. Trolley cars were stopped and negro passengers re- moved.

**1942:** During World War II, German sailors were brought to Charleston Navy Yard after their U-boat, U-352, was sunk off the coast of South Carolina.

**1950s:** Charleston was a segregated city. It had separate schools, restaurants, hotels, and neighborhoods for Black people and white people.

**1963:** As the Civil Rights Movement grew in the South and moved into South Carolina, Rev. Martin Luther King Jr. spoke at Charleston's historic Emanuel AME Church.

**1975:** Septima Poinsette Clark became the first Black woman to serve on the Charleston School Board. The daughter of an enslaved man, Clark was a big part of the Civil Rights Movement in Charleston and a longtime teacher. Winning this job capped a long life of service to Black people and Charleston's children.

**1989:** Hurricane Hugo hit Charleston and damaged twenty-five historically important buildings and many other structures, causing $7 billion of damage in the state.

## Charleston Renaissance

The years between World War I and World War II were known as the Charleston Renaissance. Charleston enjoyed a cultural "rebirth." Art, music, literature, history, and preservation took center stage to help Charleston become the cultural center it is today.

# People from the Past!

We could fill a book with amazing people from Charleston history. Here are some folks you might like to meet.

**Elizabeth Timothy (1700–1757)**

In 1738, Elizabeth Timothy became the country's first known female journalist when she took over as editor and publisher of the *South Carolina Gazette* after her husband died. The paper had been started by her husband with financial backing from Benjamin Franklin in 1733. Even though Timothy ran the paper herself, her 13-year-old son Peter's name appeared on the *Gazette's* masthead as the publisher.

**Eliza Lucas Pinckney (1722–1793)**

Eliza Lucas Pinckney developed indigo, a plant used in clothing dyes, as one of colonial Charleston's most important cash crops. Born and raised on a plantation in the Caribbean, Pinckney moved to the Lowcountry as a teenager. With her father away, Pinckney was left in charge of the family's three plantations where she was determined to find a new crop to grow. Her farm used enslaved people from the Gullah community (see page 34). Indigo became a major export, second only to rice.

**John Rutledge (1739–1800)**

Born in Charleston, Rutledge grew up to become one of its most distinguished citizens. (Plus, his brother Edward was a signer of the Declaration of Independence.) John was president of South Carolina during the American Revolution, governor of the state of South Carolina, and one of the very first justices on the United States Supreme Court (nominated by George Washington himself).

**Robert Smalls (1839-1915)**

Robert Smalls was born into slavery in Beaufort, South Carolina. During the Civil War his job was to steer a Confederate military transport ship. However, he made a daring escape from Charleston Harbor by dressing up as the ship's captain and sailing the ship out of Confederate-controlled waters and surrendering it to the Union navy. His bravery freed not only himself and fellow crew members but their families as well. Smalls went on to serve in the Union Navy and in the US House of Representatives.

# Gullah People of South Carolina

The Gullah-Geechee people live a unique African-American culture. Descended from enslaved people from African nations, they mixed and blended to create a culture that endures to this day. People from the Caribbean and other places have joined over the years, too. Art, crafts, foods, music, and Gullah language are still part of life for the Gullah people who live in the Lowcountry today.

**Language:** Gullah is a colorful mix of English, African, and Creole words. A typical Gullah greeting is ‘How huhhah fah do?” which means “How are you?” You can probably guess what some of the words mean. For instance, “chillun” means “children,” “fambly” means “family,” and “’gatuh” means alligator. Some words are totally different from their English translation. For instance, the Gullah word for rude or impolite is “nomannussubble.” A cultural commission works to make sure the language remains part of the community.

**Baskets:** Sweetgrass baskets are a Gullah tradition that has been passed down from generation to generation. They were first made in the rice fields for "fanning" rice to separate the seed from the chaff. The baskets were also used to store and carry food. Today seagrass baskets are a beloved art form. If you drive down Highway 17 in Mount Pleasant and visit the Charleston City Market, you'll find roadside stands where artists sell their baskets.

**New Foods:** Gullah people brought peanuts, okra, rice, yams, peas, hot peppers, sesame seeds, sorghum, and watermelon with them to America. Their traditional one-pot cooking style inspired famous Charleston dishes like the Perloo and Frogmore stew (above).

At the **Caw Caw Interpretive Center**, see exhibits about Gullah culture, plus take a short hike around rice fields to check out the Lowcountry wildlife.

# Charleston Weather

Weather reporters probably find Charleston boring. After all, how many ways can you say, "sunny and warm?" The pleasant weather is one of the things residents and tourists love about Charleston's subtropical climate. The area has mild winters, followed by spectacular springs. Summers, however, can be very hot and humid. Thunderstorms are common, usually in the afternoon or evening. Locals say that if you don't like the weather . . . just wait a minute!

On the other hand, the odds are pretty high that a tropical storm will pass by Charleston at least once a year. These storms usually hit in late summer or early fall between August and October and can be very dangerous.

**Snow or Storm?** Occasionally, the weather goes a little crazy in Charleston. About every five years or so the area is delighted by light snow flurries. Getting enough to cover the ground and build a snowman occurs about every ten years.

**Summer weather** gets hot and humid and is the cause of many a frizzy bad hair day. Even so, the coastal breezes blowing in over sandy beaches make for a cooler escape. And there's always plenty of sweet tea on hand to quench your thirst.

FAST FACTS

**Weather** means what it is like outside day by day. **Climate** means what the weather is like over long periods of time.

# Hurricanes Hit Home!

The National Weather Service began tracking hurricanes in 1851. Since then, they have recorded 309 tropical cyclones hitting the Charleston area. That includes tropical depressions (winds up to 38 miles per hour), tropical storms (sustained winds of 39 to 73 miles per hour), and hurricanes. The last are the worst, with circular winds of more than 74 miles per hour, rough seas, and heavy rains. They can be very destructive to property and deadly for people.

This satellite view shows a hurricane approaching South Carolina. High winds spin to form the circular rain-packed clouds.

**Hurricane Hugo** was the worst recorded hurricane to hit Charleston. It roared in from Sullivan's Island just north of the city on September 21, 1989. A category 4 storm with winds raging at up to 140 miles per hour, it sank ships, ripped roofs off homes, and snapped trees like matchsticks. Electricity was out in parts of the city for weeks. Hundreds of thousands of people had to evacuate to safer places inland. Many homes and businesses were completely destroyed. All told Hurricane Hugo caused $7 billion in damage in South Carolina.

**Gracie** In 1959, this hurricane pushed a storm surge of nine feet of water into Charleston Harbor. Boats were destroyed and ten people died. Winds of 150 miles or more swept across the city and the state, destroying buildings.

**Hazel** This 1954 hurricane killed 95 people with winds of more than 130 miles per hour.

**1885:** In the time before such storms got names, this hurricane covered many city streets with ocean water pushed in from the Atlantic over a seawall. According to one report, more than 100 people died. Other storms were recorded in 1822, 1854, and 1874. Earlier storms surely hit, too, but not as many details remain.

# IT'S OFFICIAL!

Cities and states choose a lot of different things to make "official" for their places. Here is some of the official stuff for Charleston.

## OFFICIAL CITY FLAG (SEAL):

Mayor Joseph P. Riley changed the Charleston city flag in the mid-1990s. The dark blue flag features three main images that represent 1670 (the year the city was founded), 1783 (the year the city was incorporated), and a woman (a traditional representation of the city).

## OFFICIAL CITY MOTTO:

*Ædes Mores Juraque Curat.*
This is Latin for "She Guards Her Temples, Customs, and Laws."

## REALITY CHECK!

The South Carolina state flag is much more popular than Charleston's city flag. It's partly because of the great story behind it, but mostly because the flag's image is so cool. During one of the first battles of the American Revolution, British troops attacked Charleston's Fort Sullivan. But their cannon fire was no match for Fort Sullivan. It was built with palmetto tree logs. The logs were so strong that the cannonballs pretty much bounced off them. The Redcoats were defeated and the palmetto tree made it onto the new flag.

# OFFICIAL SOUTH CAROLINA STATE STUFF

Animal: White-tailed deer

Fish: Striped bass

Marine Mammal: Bottlenose dolphin

Insect: Carolina mantis

**REPTILE:** Loggerhead sea turtle

**FLOWER:** Yellow jessamine, also known as Carolina Jasmine

**BUTTERFLY:** Tiger swallowtail

**BIRD:** Carolina wren

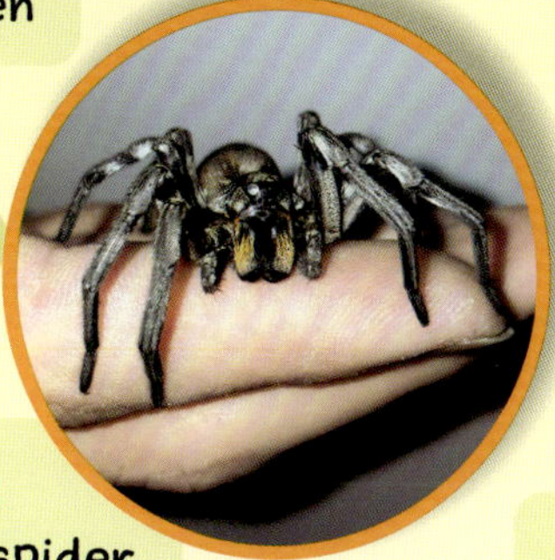

**SPIDER:** Carolina wolf spider

**DOG:** Boykin spaniel

The **Charleston Tea Garden** is the only place in North America where tea is grown. Visitors see fields with hundreds of thousands of tea bushes, tour the factory to see how tea is made, and sample both hot and cold teas.

# Things to see in Charleston

Whether exploring natural beauty, visiting great parks, or traveling back in time to Charleston's history, there are dozens and dozens of things to do when you visit.

## Angel Oak

Angel Oak, a Lowcountry treasure, is said to be the largest live oak tree east of the Mississippi River. It is estimated to be 300 to 400 years old and can be found in a city park on Johns Island.

## Shem Creek

Shem Creek is a local favorite where you can enjoy great views of the Charleston Harbor and nearby marshes, watch shrimp boats come and go, stroll along a boardwalk looking for seabirds and dolphins, and take a paddle boat or kayak out for a cruise. The area also has lots of fun restaurants.

# History Comes to Life

Charleston is famous for preserving its history. Many of the places you read about in history books (or in this book!) are still standing waiting for you to visit them.

Completed in 1713 and the oldest public building in South Carolina, the **Powder Magazine** was used to store gunpowder through the American Revolution.

**Charleston Battery:** No visit to Charleston is complete without a visit to the Battery. It's a historic defensive seawall and famous promenade. It's a toss-up whether it is more fun to see it on foot or by boat.

At the **Old Exchange and Provost Dungeon** you can find a place where George Washington threw a party, the United States Constitution was ratified, prisoners were held, and captured people were sold into slavery. Built in 1771, this historic landmark has many stories to tell.

***H.L. Hunley* Civil War Submarine:** The *H. L. Hunley* was the first successful combat submarine in history. On February 17, 1864, it sunk the mighty Union ship the USS *Housatonic* in Charleston Harbor. Then the *Hunley* wasn't seen again for 136 years. Explorers rediscovered the sunken submarine in 1995. The Hunley Lab offers weekend tours of the submarine and many of its artifacts.

**Fort Sumter** was built on a man-made island in 1829. Its purpose was to protect the valuable Charleston Harbor. It has gone down in history as the site where the Civil War began in 1861 (page 26). It is now a National Park to which visitors ferry for tours.

**Fort Moultrie,** where early colonists defeated the British, is now a National Park. The fort has been restored to show its important role throughout history from the American Revolution through World War II.

# More History!

**Plantations:** Several restored plantations provide a glimpse of long-ago life in Charleston. Most offer the perspectives of both plantation owners and enslaved people. Popular tours are available at Boone Hall Plantation, Drayton Hall, Magnolia Plantation, McLeod Plantation, and Middleton Place.

**Old Slave Market Museum:** Thought to be the only known slave auction site in South Carolina still in existence, the Old Slave Market stands as a reminder of Charleston's past as the largest slave port in the United States.

**City Market:** First opened in the 1790s, this is one of the oldest public markets in Charleston, and a great place to find food, arts and crafts, and souvenirs.

**Four Corners of Law:** Buildings on the four corners of Meeting and Broad Streets represent 1: God's law (St. Michael's Episcopal Church), 2: state law (Charleston County Courthouse), 3: city law (Charleston City Hall), and 4: federal law (Federal Courthouse).

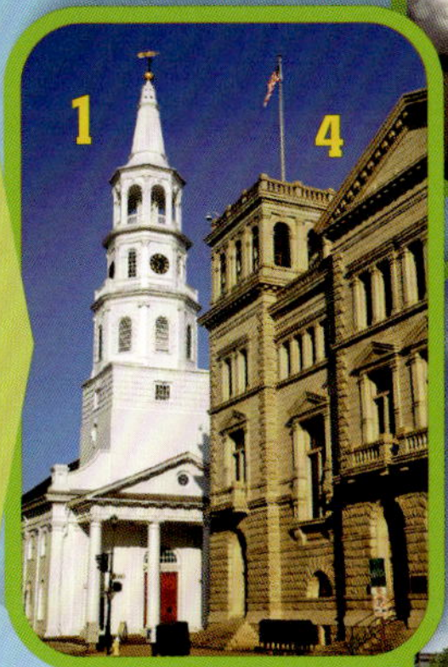

**Travel in Time:** Visit the Nathaniel Russell House (top) to see what life was like for a family (and its enslaved people) in 1808. The Aiken-Rhett House (bottom) is another restored set of buildings. Along with the main house of the Aiken family, you can see well-preserved places where enslaved people lived in the 1850s.

# Charleston Famous Firsts

Here are some times when Charleston made history by being first.

**1706 Old St. Andrew's Parish Church** is the oldest surviving church in the Carolinas.

**1736** The nation's first permanent playhouse, **Dock Street Theatre**, opened with a performance of *The Recruiting Office.*

**1773** America's first museum, The Charleston Museum, was organized.

**1773 The College of Charleston**, the nation's first municipal college was established.

**1776 The first American victory of the American Revolution in the South** was the Battle of Fort Sullivan on Sullivan's Island.

**1864 World's first successful submarine attack** when the Confederate submarine, the *H.L. Hunley*, sunk the Union ship, *Housatonic*.

**1786 America's first golf club**, South Carolina Golf Club (also known as Harleston Green), was started in Charleston.

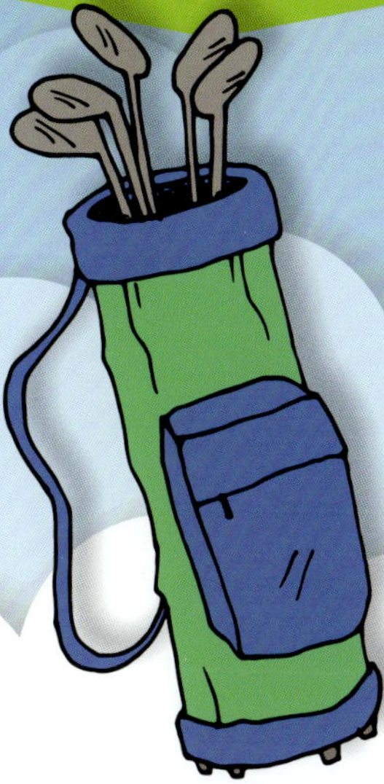

**1861 The first shots of the American Civil War** were fired from Fort Sumter.

# Beaches Galore

It is not a question of whether to go to the beach when you visit Charleston. The big question is *which* beach to visit. It's hard to go wrong when you have so many choices.

**Isle of Palms** is a slender barrier island near Charleston. It's known for beaches backed by condos and eateries. The beachfront County Park is the place to be with a picnic area and playground. Isle of Palms is a key sea turtle nesting site in the summer. Just remember, look but don't touch!

**Folly Beach** Folly Beach has a fun, family vibe and is Charleston's best place to surf. It is home to the Folly Beach Pier, which stretches more than 1,000 feet (304 m) out over the ocean. Its Center Street is lined with surf and souvenir shops. Enjoy a picnic at Folly Beach County Park and check out the pelican rookery. You can also visit the Morris Island Lighthouse nearby.

**Kiawah Island** Kiawah is the fanciest of all the Charleston beaches. Located near a world-class resort, it is a gem with ten miles of beaches, forests, sand dunes, and marshes. It's a great place to ride bikes, too. While you're there, watch for whitetail deer, alligators, seabirds, and sea turtles. It is one of the only places in the world you can see dolphins strand feeding. That is when dolphins herd a school of fish or shrimp onto a sandbar (see page 79). Then the dolphins launch their bodies out of the water for a picnic on the beach.

**Sullivan's Island** Smaller, peaceful, and beautiful, Sullivan's Island is a favorite spot for walks on the beach, watersports, and nature watching. When you tire of the surf and sun, you can soak up some Revolutionary War history at nearby Fort Moultrie. Locals hang out at an array of fun restaurants, including Poe's Tavern (named after author Edgar Allen Poe).

# GETTING AROUND CHARLESTON

Boats: With an ocean, rivers, and creeks all around them, people in Charleston spend a lot of time on the water. They ride sailboats, fishing boats, kayaks, and canoes. Tour boats take tourists out to see historic sites, dolphins, and ghosts.

DASH: Visitors to the center of town can ride free DASH shuttle buses between the major attractions and historic sites.

Bikes: With so many beautiful days to enjoy being outside, bike rides are a favorite way to see the city. Bikers pedal around downtown, on the beach (on hardpacked sand during low tide), and through beautiful parks and trails. The city has put nice green rental bikes at stands around town.

Horse and Carriage: Tours take tourists around historic downtown Charleston. Guides share fascinating facts about the city and its history, people, and architecture during the ride.

**National Outdoor Sculpture Competition and Exhibit:** Held in North Charleston, this event attracts sculptors from around the world. Even if you can't go to the actual event (usually in May), some of the top sculptures are displayed for the following year in Riverfront Park.

# Art in Charleston

Looking for art? In Charleston, just look around! There is outdoor art almost everywhere in town. Here's a quick guide to some favorites.

**Summerville in Feathers:** In Summerville, just northwest of Charleston, art has gone to the birds. The local Audubon Society coordinated work among local artists to create dozens of sculptures, large and small, of birds that can be seen nearby. The sculptures are found throughout the town, so keep a sharp lookout!

**Oyster Art:** The nearby town of Mt. Pleasant is home to some real oyster lovers. Local artists have painted and put on display four-foot tall oyster shell sculptures to honor the squishy dish.

**Marvelous Murals:** Artist David Boatwright and others have decorated walls in and around Charleston with colorful murals. Some of Boatwright's show Charleston citizens, both famous and not. Look for more murals in the Avondale neighborhood, as well as a beautiful mosaic at Romney Urban Garden.

# Museums in Charleston

With a history as varied as Charleston's, it takes more than one museum to tell its story.

Originally started as the Carolina Art Association in 1858, the **Gibbes Museum of Art** has evolved through the years. With more than 10,000 works of art, it is home to one of the largest collections of Southern art in the world. The museum's goal is to use art to "inspire our imagination, heal our hurt, and nourish our souls."

**International African American Museum:** Gadsden's Wharf is where 40 percent of enslaved Africans first arrived in America. Now it's the site of a new museum where people can explore the history of slavery, the Civil Rights Movement, and present events. (*NOTE: This museum is scheduled to open for the first time in Fall 2022.*)

**The Charleston Museum** shows that the city's history is "a blend of beauty and pain, grace and war, great stories and calm seas." The museum offers exhibits, programs, and activities that "spark a conversation not just about who we were, but who we are—and who we can be."

**The Children's Museum of the Lowcountry** is where Charleston's kids come to learn and play. Race boats down rapids, climb aboard a pirate ship, shop for make-believe groceries, and create all kinds of arts and crafts.

**Patriots Point Naval & Maritime Museum:** Tour the World War II aircraft carrier, USS *Yorktown*, see a fleet of historic ships, and check out a Cold War memorial. Just across the Ravenel bridge from Charleston, Patriots Point attracts over 300,000 visitors each year.

# Charleston on Stage

**Charleston Galliard Center:** The Galliard is where Charleston goes for big-name concerts, Broadway shows, dance performances, and classical music. The beautiful theater also hosts many Spoleto Festival events.

The **North Charleston Coliseum and Performing Arts Center** is the area's largest entertainment venue. It is a convention center, arena, and theater all in one. It hosts everything from Broadway plays to South Carolina Stingray hockey games. It's the go-to place for the biggest names in music and all kinds of trade shows and expos.

**Dock Street Theatre:** The original location of this building was the site of the first theatrical performances in the thirteen colonies. In 1735, it was also the site of the first opera performance in America. The original building was destroyed by the Great Fire of 1740. The current building opened in 1809 and is still delighting people with many performances each year.

The **Palmetto City Ballet** is Charleston's only professional ballet company. It focuses on performances, dance training, and community education. They often perform at the College of Charleston's Sottile Theatre.

## Spoleto Festival USA

Charleston hosted its first Spoleto Festival in 1977. Since then, the event has grown to be one of the most spectacular performing arts events in America. For more than two weeks each summer, Charleston entertains thousands of guests with opera, theater, dance, and music performances across the city.

# Celebrate! Charleston Style

Pick a weekend . . . (almost) any weekend! There is likely to be some sort of festival or event to enjoy in Charleston.

The **Lowcountry Oyster Festival** is held in January at the Boone Hall Plantation. The main event is eating lots and lots of oysters—more than 80,000 pounds of 'em. Thankfully, there are lots of people on hand to help shuck 'em!

**2nd Sunday on King:** On the second Sunday of each month, King Street is blocked off to cars, and people come to shop, eat, and celebrate.

**Festival of Houses and Gardens:** In spring, beautiful private homes and gardens in Charleston open their doors to visitors, thanks to the Historical Charleston Foudation. There are tours, lectures, and special events that celebrate Charleston's historic charm.

Each spring, the **Credit One Charleston Open**—the oldest and largest all-women's tennis tournament in North America—comes to CHS.

The **Southeastern Wildlife Exposition** (SEWE), is a celebration of the great outdoors. It happens every February and brings together artists, craftspeople, collectors, and sports fans to connect over a shared passion for wildlife. SEWE events include concerts and art exhibits, as well as dog competitions and bird-of-prey demos.

# Charleston Speaks

As Southerners, Charleston natives often have a colorful way of expressing themselves. Here are some words and phrases heard around town.

### Hissy fit

**Temper tantrum**

### Pluff mud

**Gooey marsh mud that lines the Lowcountry; many Charleston natives say it "smells like home"**

### "Give me some sugar"

**Give me a kiss**

### Palmetto bugs

**Better known as the American cockroach (and also called water bugs), they thrive (and gross people out) in Charleston's hot and humid climate**

## Buggy

The cart you push around a grocery store

## Crank

Start the car

## *Charleston Shuffle*

The "dance" people do when they shuffle or trip on downtown's many brick sidewalks.

## Frogmore stew

Soupy dish made from shrimp, sausage, corn, and potatoes but, thank heavens, no frogs

# What People Do in CHARLESTON

### Tourism

In a typical year, Charleston greets more than seven million visitors who spend close to $950 million per year for lodging. That adds up to a lot of jobs in tourism in Charleston! That includes everyone who works in restaurants and hotels as well as those who run tour businesses, own souvenir shops, and so much more.

### Education

With several colleges and growing numbers of private and public schools for students of all ages, many educators pursue careers in Charleston.

## Manufacturing

Lots of stuff gets made in Charleston, including Boeing aircraft, Mercedes Benz vans, Volvo sedans, boats, flight simulators, automobile parts, and the list goes on. Why so much "making"? See the next box!

## Shipping

Charleston is a big shipping hub so all the products made here then make their way to places around the world for people to buy. Ships, trains, and trucks—Charleston has a world-class transportation system that supports imports and exports.

## Health Care

Taking care of people is big business in Charleston, with almost 40,000 people working in the health care industry. The biggest employers are the Medical University of South Carolina (MUSC), Roper St. Francis, and Trident Health Care systems.

# Hey! I'm from Charleston, too!

**Reese Witherspoon**

This popular actress and producer is another "import," born in New Orleans but now living in Charleston. She starred in movies and shows like *Legally Blonde*, *Big Little Lies*, and *Wild*. She says that Charleston is one of her all-time favorite southern cities, and she has a home on Sullivan's Island.

**Bill Murray**

Bill Murray was born in Illinois, but the famous actor, comedian, and writer has made himself at home in Charleston. He is especially well-known for his work on *Saturday Night Live* and in the Ghostbuster movies. Murray is part-owner of the RiverDogs, Charleston's minor league baseball team.

**Darius Rucker**

The award-winning country singer and Hootie and the Blowfish star grew up in Charleston and has a home there. Every year his band plays a concert to raise money for local Charleston schools. He has also been a generous supporter of the Medical University of South Carolina (MUSC) Children's Hospital and Women's Pavilion, where his mother worked for 30 years.

**Vanessa Lachey**

She spent part of her childhood in Charleston and went to school there before becoming a TV star (*NCIS Hawaii* and other shows). Lachey was selected as Miss South Carolina Teen USA and went on to win the Miss Teen USA pageant in 1998.

# Eating in Charleston

Like most places, Charleston has some food items that are "locals only." But of course you're welcome to try them out when you visit!

**Barbecue:** Parts of South Carolina are known as the Mustard Belt because, unlike vinegar-based North Carolina barbecue, the tangy meat sauces in South Carolina often include mustard! Pork is the favorite type of barbecue in Charleston restaurants, no matter what the sauce is.

**Fried green tomatoes:** Just what it says: Take green tomatoes (not fully ripe). Slice 'em, fry 'em, eat 'em.

**Sweet tea:** When you get tea in Charleston, it's going to be cold, on ice, and packed with sugar. Tea is not just for breakfast anymore!

**Shrimp and grits:** Shrimp you know; grits you might not. They are the official food of the state of South Carolina, and are a tasty porridge-like mix of cornmeal and grains. Mix grits with shrimp and you get a Charleston favorite.

**Hushpuppies:** What's tastier than fried dough? Not much. These Southern favorites are made from a cornmeal batter, rolled up, and fried. Eat them with barbecued meat or just about anything! Some folks like them with a little syrup.

## Kids' Favorite Charleston Restaurants

* Have some sandbox fun and climb aboard a vintage truck while munching wood-fired pizza at **Coastal Crust** (at Vintage Coffee Café).
* Looking for the best macaroni and cheese? Try **Cru Café**. Located in a classic 18th century Charleston single-style home, it offers a true Charleston dining experience.
* Sullivan's Island's **Middle Street** is the place to go for dining at the beach. Find tacos and BBQ to seafood and ice-cream treats.
* Save room for dessert! Get a big bowl of banana pudding, a slice of pecan pie, or a chunk of coconut cake at **Kaminsky's Dessert Café** (right).

# Go, Charleston Sports!

Baseball has been big in Charleston since right after the Civil War. From 1866 to 1886 there were over 100 individual Black and white baseball clubs playing in town. Baseball mania got really real in 1886 when the Charleston Seagulls, Charleston's first professional baseball team, came to town. Their first season ended abruptly when a major earthquake shook things up on August 31.

## CHARLESTON RIVERDOGS

**Play** in the Carolina League

- The RiverDogs play minor-league pro baseball.
- Started play in 1994 as the Royals and later the Rainbow.
- Formerly part of the New York Yankees organization.
- Co-owned by actor Bill Murray (right).

**Home:** Joseph P. Riley Park

## SOUTH CAROLINA STINGRAYS

**Play** in the East Coast Hockey League

- The Stingrays play minor-league pro hockey.
- Began play in 1993.
- The mascot is named Cool Ray.

**Home:** North Charleston Coliseum

**No one knows for sure, but the name of the hockey puck supposedly came from a character in Shakespeare's "A Midsummer's Night Dream"**

**Charleston Swings It**

As the home of America's very first golf club, it's no surprise that golf is still a popular sport in Charleston. Players take their pick of dozens of golf courses and play almost all year in the city's mild weather. Nearby Kiawah is home to five championship courses, including all the seaside holes at the Ocean Course.

# Active Charleston!

Now that you know where to watch sports in Charleston, how about where you go to play some! With great weather and lots of open space on land and water, Charleston is packed with active things to do.

**Cooper River Bridge Run** Some people see a bridge and want to drive over it. In Charleston, they see the Cooper River Bridge . . . and want to run over it! The long bridge is part of an annual 10-kilometer race that attracts nearly 40,000 runners!

**Charleston Race Week** With great winds for sailing, boats of all shapes and sizes, plus talented sailing crews, Charleston Race Week is a great spring event. It started in 1996, and includes races in more than a dozen types of sailing craft.

**Charleston Water Week** With so much water in and around the city, doing fun things on the wet stuff is a big deal here. Each September, thousands of people get out and get wet during Charleston Water Week. Events include kitesurfing, paddleboarding, canoeing, parasailing, swimming, windsurfing, and much more.

**Fishing** What lives in all this water around Charleston? Fish. Fishing fans of all ages can drop a line in creeks, rivers, streams, ponds, lakes, and of course the ocean. A big species of bass known as Red Drum is one of the favorites to aim for. You can also haul in spotted seatrout, black sea bass, king mackerel, and many more. Few places have the variety of fishing experiences that Charleston does.

**Charleston Classic** College basketball teams often play in mini-tournaments to get ready for the regular season. Since 2008, teams have been coming to such an event in Charleston. Local fans get to watch superstars of the court, often including local schools, including the College of Charleston and fellow South Carolina school Clemson.

# COLLEGE TOWN

Colleges and universities old and new can be found in Charleston. Maybe you can head there for a degree someday.

## COLLEGE OF CHARLESTON

**Founded** 1770

**Students:** 10,667

**Popular majors:** Historic Preservation and Community Planning, Latin American and Caribbean Studies, Public Health, Supply Chain Management

**Fast Fact:** College of Charleston is older than the United States!

## CHARLESTON SOUTHERN UNIVERSITY

**Founded** 1964

**Students**: 3,349

**Popular majors:** Aeronautics, Christian Studies, Entrepreneurship, Global Marketplace, Ministry

**Fast Fact:** Charleston Southern is the Lowcountry's only Christian university.

Charleston Southern University main chapel

## THE CITADEL MILITARY COLLEGE OF SOUTH CAROLINA

**Founded** 1842
**Students**: 3,300
**Popular majors:** Civil Engineering, Construction Engineering, Criminal Justice, Cyber Operations, Intelligence and Security Studies
**Fast Fact:** Citadel cadets performed military duties for the Confederates during the Civil War.

## MEDICAL UNIVERSITY OF SOUTH CAROLINA (MUSC)

**Founded** 1824
**Students:** More than 3,000 students and 850 residents
**Popular majors:** Six colleges offer programs for Dental Medicine, Graduate Students, Health Professions, Medicine, Nursing, and Pharmacy.
**Fast Fact:** Students get hands-on training at MUSC hospital, which is often voted the best hospital in South Carolina.

## TRIDENT TECHNICAL COLLEGE

**Founded** 1973
**Students:** 12,000
**Popular majors:** Culinary and Hospitality, Engineering and Manufacturing, Maintenance and Technical Trades, University Transfer
**Fast Fact:** Many students earn their two-year associate degree at Trident Tech and then transfer to a university for further study.

# Time for Play and Picnics!

**Battery Park and White Point Gardens**
With the Charleston Harbor on one side, beautiful antebellum mansions on another, and Fort Sumter in the distance, White Point Gardens offers a one-of-kind Charleston experience. It's perfect for pleasant walks to see all the flower boxes and picnics overlooking the sea.

**Marion Square** is located in the middle of downtown Charleston. There's always something fun happening there. Saturdays are Farmer's Market Days, while it's also home to Charleston Fashion Week and Spoleto Festival events. College of Charleston students play frisbee or study in the sun here.

**Charles Towne Landing** This is the spot where Charleston got its start. Now it's like walking back into colonial times, complete with bike rentals, nature and history trails, and 80 acres of gardens and greenery. A bonus is the natural habitat for animal species that shared this land with the early settlers.

**Charleston Waterfront Park** Famous for its Pineapple Fountain (the pineapple is a symbol of Southern hospitality), this is Charleston's most popular park, with great views of the Charleston Harbor. Watch for sailboats and large cargo ships coming in and out of the harbor.

# Sea Creatures

With so much ocean saltwater and fresh waterways, Charleston is a haven for all kinds of sea creatures.

**Alligators** are very common in Charleston. They hang out in freshwater and can be found in rivers, marshes, ponds, canals, and even in golf course lakes. People often spot alligators sunning themselves or floating in the water.

## Gator Rules

- **Keep your distance and do not approach alligators,** even if they are just lazing around in the sun.
- **Never ever feed an alligator.** It is a danger to them and to humans.
- **Do not swim in areas where alligators tend to live.** Splashing around on their turf is like saying "hello, dinner is here" to an alligator.

**Dolphins:** Dolphins tend to travel in groups. These playful flippered friends are a delight to watch in action. Experts estimate that more than 300 resident dolphins call the Charleston area home. Some of the most popular places to spot them are Shem Creek, the Lighthouse Inlet on Folly Beach, Bulls Island, and Charleston Harbor.

## Dolphin Strand Feeding

For pure dolphin magic, watching a strand feeding is a must. Strand feeding is when dolphins push themselves onto the beach after herding a tasty meal of fish and shrimp onshore. They chase the "meal" onto a sandbar or mudflat, then gobble it up. It all happens in a matter of seconds and usually happens in the two hours before and after low tide. The best spot to see a strand feeding is Captain Sam's Inlet, a spot that separates Kiawah from Seabrook Island. Strand feeding is only known to occur in a very few places around the world.

Where else can people "sea" over 5,000 animals and visit a Sea Turtle Care Center? **The South Carolina Aquarium** is a popular destination for an up-close look at South Carolina's native animals and plants—from the mountains to the coast. You can find ideas to help protect the planet with opportunities for citizen science, plastic pollution prevention, and more.

# Sea Turtle Wonders

In one of the most spectacular events in nature, female loggerhead turtles make an epic journey from their ocean homes to the place they were born in South Carolina. Once they arrive, they lay eggs and return to the sea. Those journeys can often be 8,000 miles or more! Here's what happens:

A female sea turtle uses her back flippers to dig a nest in the sand. Then she lays about 100 eggs before dragging herself back to the ocean for the long journey back.

## How to Be a Sea Turtle Superhero

➤ **Keep pets away from nests** where they might be tempted to "taste" the eggs.
➤ **Turn off lights near the beach** and keep it dark from sundown to sun up during the months of May through October.
➤ **Fill in large holes dug at the beach,** so mama turtles and their babies don't fall in.
➤ **Clean up** chairs, tents, toys, and all litter after a day at the beach.

The eggs incubate in the warm sand for about 60 days.

After about 60 days, all the sea turtles in a nest hatch at once. It makes for a bit of commotion in the nest that's called a "turtle boil."

Once hatched, the turtles make a run for the sea. The downward slope of the beach and the reflections of the moon and stars on the water guide them. Scientists think the turtles usually move at night for safety from predators.

## Human Help

SEA TURTLE PATROL
HILTON HEAD ISLAND

In popular nesting sites like the Isle of Palms, Kiawah Island, Seabrook Island, and Folly Beach, human sea turtle patrols protect the nests from people and predators. People also guard the tiny baby turtles as they make the dangerous run from beach to the ocean. Sea birds and other creatures would otherwise feast on the babies. The danger continues when the little critters enter the ocean where they are still easy pickings for predators. It's hard to say how many baby turtles survive. Experts put the odds at between 1 in 1,000 to 1 in 10,000. Those that do make it to adulthood can live between 50 and 100 years.

# Coastal Birds

Charleston's coastal areas are home to many beautiful beach birds.

**Brown pelicans** are large water birds. They eat up to four pounds of fish a day. Pelicans can spot a fish from 60 feet above the waves. They plunge-dive for food at speeds up to 40 miles per hour. They have air sacs in their necks that inflate like mini air bags when they hit the water headfirst.

**Piping plovers** are chubby, sandy colored shorebirds. They live in the Lowcountry year-round.

**Sandpipers** are the little birds commonly seen running near the water's edge on beaches and tidal mud flats. Tempting as it may be to chase them, leave the little guys be. They need to save up every ounce of energy for a long flight south for the winter.

Messy black feathers give **royal terns** a cute bed-head look. With white bodies and bold orange beaks, they forage for food just below the surface of the water. Shrimp and crab are favorite foods on their menu.

**Wood storks**, also known as wood ibis, are big birds. They stand three feet tall and have a five-foot wingspan. Their bald heads, long, grey, down-turned beaks, and black wing tips, make them easy to spot.

**Wet, grassy marsh areas are great places to see birds.**

Very active colonies of seabirds nest in the Charleston area. The birds include pelicans, terns, skimmers, and gulls, all of which gather in groups of hundreds of thousands! They tend to avoid places with lots of humans and stay close to food sources.

**Roseate spoonbills** are colorful pink birds with spoon-shaped bills. Once rare, these birds have made a comeback in the Lowcountry. You might say they are like birds of feather because they are very social. They fly in formation and nest with their heron, ibis, and stork "friends."

# CHARLESTON BY THE NUMBERS

Stats and facts and digits . . . galore! Here are some of the numbers that make Charleston what it is.

**In 2018, Charleston welcomed**

**7,300,000**

**visitors to the city.**

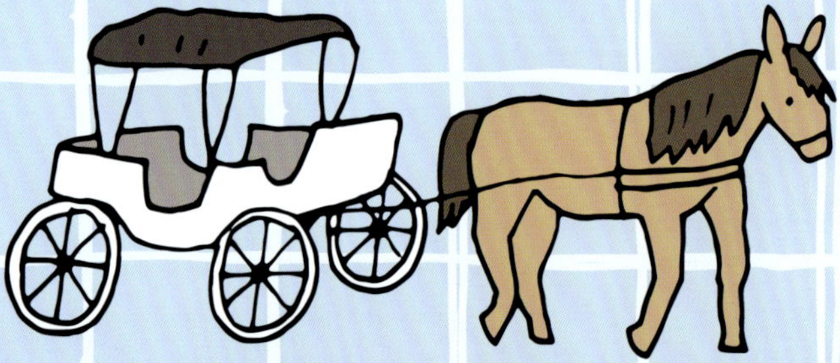

## NO. 1!

**In 2016, a national travel magazine voted Charleston as the No. 1 city . . . in the WORLD! It had already been voted No. 1 in the US but got a promotion that year.**

**More than 40,000 carriage tours roll through the city of Charleston each year. Talk about numbers . . . One 1,000-pound horse produces about 31 pounds of solid waste per day. That's about 12 tons per year. No matter how you run those numbers, that's a lot of poop to scoop!**

An average of **33** people move to the Charleston area every day.

About **100,000** alligators live in South Carolina. Many of them lurk in Charleston-area fresh waterways.

**FAST FACT**
One shipping container is big enough to hold two cars or enough produce to fill two grocery store aisles.

Cargo ships that sail in and out of Charleston ports carry as many as **24,000** 20-foot containers.

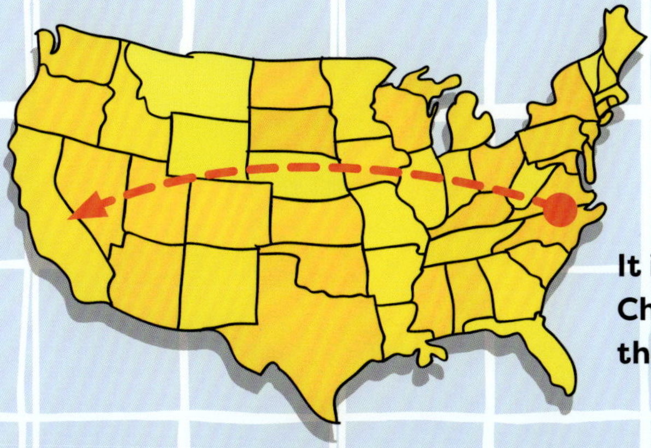

It is **2,505** miles from Charleston Harbor to the Port of Los Angeles.

# Creepy Charleston

They say that Charleston is one of the most haunted cities in America. With more than 300 years of wars, pirates, and enslaved people, there are bound to be plenty of restless spirits running around town.

**Old City Jail:** Lavinia Fisher was the first known female serial killer in America. In 1820, she was executed in Charleston—wearing her wedding dress. Some have reported seeing the spirit of the murderous bride hanging around the Old City Jail.

**Poogan's Porch:** This popular Charleston restaurant was once home to a friendly puppy named Poogan. He died in 1979. Ever since then some guests swear they've felt him brush past their legs as they eat dinner in the restaurant.

**Old Exchange and Provost Building:** Isaac Hayne was said to be a British soldier who defected to the colonists during the American Revolution. He was captured and executed by the Redcoats (the British). Sometimes people see a man dressed in Revolutionary War garb and mistake him for a guide. When he mysteriously disappears before their eyes, they are quite sure they've seen a ghost!

**Boone Hall Plantation:** At least this ghost is compassionate—there have been frequent sightings of a soldier ghost removing a bullet from his fallen comrade.

**Dock Street Theatre:** This historic place is considered the most haunted place in Charleston. Most famous of the resident ghosts is the spirit of actor Junius Brutus Booth. He was the father of John Wilkes Booth, the man who assassinated Abraham Lincoln.

**White Point Garden:** Fifty pirates were hanged at this site overlooking the Charleston Harbor in the early 1700s. If any place had a reason to be haunted, this would surely be it.

# Not Far Away

Charleston is a great place to visit, but there are some other spots to check out. You'll probably need the family car, but these destinations are worth the trip!

Time to get my toes in the sand!

Where are you?

We drove about two hours north to **Myrtle Beach**!

Looks great! How was the water?

It was pretty warm, actually! There are miles and miles of beautiful beaches here.

Splish, splash!

Wait, there's more! We found an amusement park with tons of rides.

Up, up in the air! Nice!

It was fun! There are roller coasters, too, and an aquarium. My dad even got to play some golf!

Fore!

We're going to try paddleboarding tomorrow and then find some music to listen to.

Wish I was there!

Other direction! This time we headed south to another beachy place. Hello, **Hilton Head**!

I won't ask if there's a Hilton Feet!

😄Ha! No, this is on Hilton Head Island, which has lots of beaches and resorts and hotels.

Sounds pretty nice!

It is! We started at the harbor where we saw some nice boats and this famous lighthouse.

Did you get out on the water?

Yes! We did a tour in these two-person pedal boats, and we saw dolphins right near us!

Awesome!

The whole area is beautiful, with lots of places to hike.

Did you bring your football?

Not THAT kind of hike, goofy! 😄 We saw this heron nesting in a waterway behind the island.

Looks pretty pleasant!

We also took a horseback ride on the beach and (no surprise) my dad played more golf. While he did that, we went to a great children's museum called the Sandbox.

Nice name for a place on the beach!

# Sister Cities Around the World

Charleston has sister cities on continents around the world. These sister cities share special relationships and support each other in trade and tourism.

## Sister Cities in Action

Here are some examples of how Charleston is working with and helping its sister cities:

**Spoleto:** It's no surprise these two are sister cities. After all, Charleston is home to the American version of the famous Italian arts and culture festival held here. The first one in Italy was in 1957. The South Carolina event started in 1977.

**Panama City:** The College of Charleston often hosts study abroad programs in this Central American city. Students take classes in Panama City and get the chance to visit the nearby Panama Canal.

**Freetown:** This city was founded in 1792 as a place for formerly enslaved people to build new lives after they escaped to Canada or England. Today's Freetown citizens are playing a part in helping to develop the new International African-American Museum in Charleston.

# FIND OUT MORE!

## Books, Websites, and More!

### Books


Alberti, Enigma. ***Spy on History: Mary Bowser and the Civil War Spy Ring.*** Workman, 2016.

Brown, Alphonso. ***A Gullah Guide to Charleston: Walking Through History.*** The History Press, 2008.

Cousteau, Philippe. ***Follow the Moon Home: A Tale of One Idea, Twenty Kids, and a Hundred Sea Turtles.*** Chronicle 2016.

Hill, Laban Carrick. ***Dave the Potter: Artist, Poet, Slave.*** Little Brown, 2010.

Jenrette, Cathy. ***G is for Gibbes: A Museum ABC Book.*** Gibbes Museum, 2019.

Jones-Radgawski, Jehan. ***The Escape of Robert Smalls.*** Capstone, 2019.

Monroe, Mary Alice. ***The Islanders.*** Aladdin, 2021.

Singer, Allison. ***The Ghostly Tales of Charleston.*** Arcadia, 2020.

Theis-Raven, Margot. ***Circle Unbroken.*** NY: Squarefish, 2007.

## Web Sites

**Explore Charleston**
https://www.charlestoncvb.com

**South Carolina Aquarium**
https://scaquarium.org

**Things to Do in Charleston with Kids**
https://freetoursbyfoot.com/charleston-with-kids

**Visit Charleston**
https://www.charleston.com

## Photo Credits and Thanks

Photos from Dreamstime, Library of Congress, National Park Service, Shutterstock, or Wikimedia except: North Wind Picture Archive/Alamy Stock Photo. 18 main. AP Photos: 31 TR; 34 main: Josh Galemore/ Savannah Morning News; 35 top: Bruce Smith; 38 BL Lou Krasky; 39 BR Clifton Guthrie; 72 Mic Smith. Historic Charleston Foundation: 47 B (2). U.S. Navy photo by Mass Communication Specialist 2nd Class Natalia Murillo 30 TL. Children's Museum of the Lowcountry 56 BR. Gaillard Center 58 TL..

Artwork: Lemonade Pixel; Maps (6-7) by Jessica Nevins.
Cover typography by Swell Type.

Thanks to our pal Nancy Ellwood, Kait Leggett, and the fine folks at Arcadia Children's Books!

# INDEX

# Thanks for Visiting

# CHARLESTON

Come Back Soon!